MAGGIE AND MAX

Don't miss any of these other stories by Ellen Miles!

THE PUPPY PLACE

Goldie
Snowball
Shadow
Rascal
Buddy
Flash
Scout
Patches
Noodle
Pugsley
Princess
Maggie and Max

TAYLOR-MADE TALES

The Dog's Secret
The Pirate's Plot
The Cowgirl's Luck
The Penguin's Peril

SCHOLASTIC JUNIOR CLASSICS

Doctor Dolittle
The Pied Piper
The Twelve Dancing Princesses
The Wind in the Willows

THE PUPPY PLACE

MAGGIE AND MAX

ELLEN MILES

SCHOLASTIC INC.

New York   Toronto   London   Auckland   Sydney
Mexico City   New Delhi   Hong Kong   Buenos Aires

No part of this publication may be reproduced, stored in a retrieval system, or transmitted in any form or by any means, electronic, mechanical, photocopying, recording, or otherwise, without written permission of the publisher. For information regarding permisson, write to Scholastic Inc., Attention: Permissions Department, 557 Broadway, New York, NY 10012.

ISBN-13: 978-0-545-03456-2
ISBN-10: 0-545-03456-6

Cover art by Tim O'Brien
Designed by Steve Scott

12 11 10 9 8   10 11 12/0

Printed in the U.S.A.

First printing, November 2007

For homeless families everywhere,
and for those who help them.

And to my mother, Betty,
with many thanks and much love.

CHAPTER ONE

"Eatalotta, eatalotta, eatalotta pizza!"

"Pepperoni, mushrooms, anchovies on the pizza!"

"Mozzarella cheese and Parmesan, too!"

"Mmmm, mmmm, good!"

Charles shouted happily with the group. He loved the pizza chant. He loved his bright yellow T-shirt. He loved working toward his Wolf rank. In fact, Charles loved just about everything about being in Cub Scouts.

It was cool that his best friend, Sammy, was in his den. It was awesome that they would both soon become Wolves. And Charles thought it was most especially super-cool *and* awesome that his mom and dad were Akelas — that is, den leaders.

That meant that all six Cub Scouts in Charles's den came to the Petersons' house for their meeting every week, and it also meant that both Mom and Dad came along to the Scouts' monthly pack meeting.

After Charles's dad finished leading the pizza chant, his mom shooed the pack out to the backyard so they could practice for the "Feats of Skill" they would have to perform as part of their Wolf Badge requirements. Some of the den members had a hard time sitting still for very long. So there was always time for jumping and running during their meetings.

Charles and Sammy were practicing their forward and backward rolls when Charles looked up and saw a furry brown face watching from a window in the house. "Hi, Buddy!" he yelled, waving to his puppy.

Charles loved Buddy so much. More than ice cream, more than Cub Scouts, maybe even more than Christmas, which was only a few weeks away. Buddy was brown, with a white heart-shaped patch on his chest. He was the cutest, smartest, funniest, softest, sweetest puppy ever, and — best of all — he belonged to the Petersons forever and ever.

Lots of puppies had come and gone since the Petersons had started being a foster family. (That meant that they took care of puppies who needed homes.) Usually, each puppy only stayed for a few weeks, until the Petersons found it the perfect forever home. But Buddy was different. Buddy had come to stay.

Now, in the upstairs window, another little face popped up next to Buddy's. That was the Bean, Charles's little brother. (His name was really Adam, but nobody *ever* called him that.) The Bean had a fuzzy green stuffed turtle hanging from his mouth. Mr. Turtle came from the pet store, and he had a squeaker inside. He was really a toy for dogs, not for little boys. But the Bean was not exactly a regular little boy. The Bean loved to pretend that he was a dog.

Then a third face popped up. It was Lizzie, Charles's older sister. She was keeping an eye on Buddy and the Bean while the den had its meeting. Charles figured that Lizzie was probably a little jealous of all the special time he got with Mom and Dad during Scout meetings, and of all the fun things the Scouts got to do, like crafts and skits and games.

Sure enough, Lizzie stuck her tongue out at Charles. He stuck his out back at her. Lizzie put her pinkies in the corners of her mouth and pulled it into a jack-o'-lantern shape. Charles did the same back at her. Charles was thinking about trying a new face with crossed eyes and a dangling tongue, but just then he heard Mom's voice.

"Okay, Scouts, let's head inside!" Mom was by the back door, waving her arms. "Our visitor has arrived and it's time to sit down and put on our listening ears."

The den often had special visitors. Most of the time they talked about their jobs or about how the Scouts could make a difference in the community. Last month, the chief of police had come! He had made all the Scouts "official deputies." That was cool.

Back in the living room, Dad was standing next to the Christmas tree talking to a tall man with a big, round stomach. Dad must have said something funny, because just as Charles and the others came in, the man burst into a loud, happy laugh. Dad was laughing, too.

But both men got more serious once the Scouts had settled down and were sitting in a circle on the floor. "Boys, this is Mr. Baker," Dad said, introducing the man. "He is the director of the Nest, which is a shelter for families who need temporary homes."

"You mean, like the way we take care of puppies?" Charles asked.

Dad nodded. "Sort of. Does everybody remember the big fire at Pinewood Apartments last week?"

Charles nodded along with all the other boys. He sure did remember. He remembered Dad's beeper going off in the middle of dinner. Dad was a fireman, and he was always ready to go in an emergency. He'd had to leave right away to help with the Pinewood fire, and it had kept him busy until very late that night.

"Fortunately, nobody was hurt by that fire," Mr. Baker said. "But three families lost their homes. So they are staying with us at the Nest. We have two other families staying there, too. Families that need a little help. With five families, we're full to the brim."

Sammy raised his hand. "How long do the people stay?"

"Usually only for a month or two," answered

Mr. Baker. "Just until they get back on their feet. Sometimes a mom or dad needs some help with finding a job, or with learning English if they are from another country. We can help with that. We also help the kids with their homework, and make sure they get to school every day."

Now another Scout spoke up. "Do the families help out at the Nest?"

"They sure do," said Mr. Baker. "We all work together to keep the Nest going, just like you all help out with chores at home. In return, the families get a safe, warm place to live and three meals a day until they can find new homes."

Now Mom spoke up. "Three *delicious* meals," she said. "I had dinner there once when I was writing an article about the Nest." Charles's mom was a reporter for the *Littleton News,* the local newspaper.

"We do have a good cook," agreed Mr. Baker. "And I must admit I enjoy helping out in the kitchen, too. I wonder if you boys can guess what kind of things I like to make? I'll give you a hint: My name says it all."

Charles got the hint. "Cookies!" he yelled.

"Cake!" yelled Sammy.

"That's right, I'm a baker," said Mr. Baker. "And when you come to the Nest next week, you can sample some of my treats."

Dad spoke up again. "Remember how we agreed at our last meeting that we wanted to volunteer somewhere, to help others in our community? Well, Mr. Baker has invited us to help serve dinner at the Nest one night a week for the next month. We'll even be there for Christmas Eve!"

Mr. Baker was nodding and smiling. "We can't wait to have you," he said. "Especially on Christmas Eve. That's when we put on our annual showcase — you know, singing, dancing, all that stuff. And our volunteers are the stars of the show!"

Charles gulped. Working at the Nest sounded

like fun, and it would be great to help people on Christmas Eve. But, performing in front of a group of people was *not* his idea of a good time. Just the thought of it made his hands feel all hot and sweaty. But there wasn't time to worry about that now. It was time to say good-bye to Mr. Baker and finish up their meeting with a song. Mom turned out all the lights except for the ones on the Christmas tree. Then Charles and the other Scouts sang "Show Akela we stand tall, we are Cub Scouts after all" to the tune of "It's a Small World After All." Singing was fun, as long as it wasn't for an audience.

They were on the last verse when Charles heard the phone ring. A moment later, Lizzie rushed into the room. "Ms. Dobbins just called!" she said to Mom. "She wants us to come over right away. She says she needs a foster family *tonight*."

Ms. Dobbins was the director of Caring Paws,

the animal shelter where Lizzie volunteered one day a week. Ms. Dobbins and her staff took care of lots of dogs and cats, but sometimes they needed help. That's where the Petersons came in.

As soon as the last Cub Scout had been picked up by his parents, the Petersons piled into their van and headed for Caring Paws. When they arrived at the animal shelter, Ms. Dobbins greeted them at the door. Without wasting any time, she led them into the building and down the hall. Charles thought they were going to the dog room, but instead she brought them into her office. There, in the corner, was an enormous cardboard box. It was wrapped in bright green shiny paper, and a big, red, floppy bow hung down one side.

"Look what just arrived," said Ms. Dobbins. "I was working late and I didn't even hear a car pull up, but when I went to lock the front door I found this box on the steps."

Charles, Lizzie, and the Bean moved closer to

the box and peeked inside. Their parents were right behind them.

Charles caught a glimpse of a wide, shaggy, white-and-brown face with big eyes that looked like melted chocolate looking up at him. A puppy! A puppy with floppy brown ears and a long feathery tail and the biggest paws Charles had ever seen.

"Wow!" Dad was staring into the box. "That is one *huge* puppy!"

"Ohh!" said Lizzie. "How cute! Is it a Saint Bernard?"

"Uppy!" whispered the Bean, who had to stand on his tiptoes to look into the box.

"Keep looking," said Ms. Dobbins.

"Oh, my!" said Mom suddenly. "There's a kitten in there, too!"

CHAPTER TWO

"Exactly." Ms. Dobbins crossed her arms and nodded. "There's a kitten, too. Can you beat that?"

"But — who brought them here?" Charles wanted to know. He could barely take his eyes off the big dog and the tiny kitten. The kitten was black, with white whiskers, a white chest; it had three white feet and one black one.

"That's a mystery," Ms. Dobbins said. "A mystery that will never be solved, I'm afraid. But whoever it was, I'm sure they did the right thing. Maybe they weren't able to take care of these animals, but they knew we would be able to help. There was a note on the box, but all it said was 'Please take care of Maggie and Max.' The puppy is a girl, so she must be Maggie."

"And you must be Max." Charles was looking down at the kitten. The kitten stared back at Charles with green eyes that were almost too big for his face. Then he opened his little pink mouth and let out a long, pitiful meow.

Help me, pleeease!

Charles felt his heart swell up. Right away, he knew he would do *anything* for that little kitten.

Maggie the puppy seemed to feel the same way. She put her big face down and gave the kitten a long, slurpy lick.

Don't you worry, dear little friend. I'm right here.

Max gave another, softer meow and settled down, curling up between Maggie's paws.

"You see how it is," said Ms. Dobbins. "These two are obviously old friends. I tried to separate them, but when I put Max in the cat room he just cried and cried and cried. And Maggie seemed to be able to hear him from all the way down the hall in the dog room! She barked and barked and begged to be let out of her cage. Finally I brought them both in here, and they calmed down."

"Whoa! Hold on there." Dad held up both hands. "Don't tell me you're asking us to take *both* of them!"

Ms. Dobbins just nodded. "That's exactly what I'm asking. How can I keep them here? I don't want to separate them, and I can't put a kitten in the dog room or a puppy — especially a puppy this big! — in the cat room."

"Well, with Christmas so close and so much to do for the holidays, I just don't think —" Dad began.

"We'll take them!" interrupted Mom. While Dad and Ms. Dobbins were talking, Mom had reached into the box to pick up the kitten, and now she was holding Max up to her cheek and kissing his soft little face. Maggie the puppy watched closely, with worried eyes.

Charles was surprised. "Really?" he asked.

Mom hardly even seemed to hear him. She just nodded dreamily as she whispered baby talk to the kitten.

Lizzie shrugged. "Mom always was more of a cat person," she reminded Charles.

Dad was shrugging, too. And grinning. "Okay!" he told Ms. Dobbins. "I guess that settles it. We're taking them!"

The Bean cheered and started to hop all around Ms. Dobbins's office. "Uppy! Uppy! Kitty! Uppy!" he sang, waving his fists in the air. "Yay! Yay! Yay!"

Charles felt like singing and hopping, too.

Instead, he helped Dad and Ms. Dobbins by opening the door while they carried the big box out to the Petersons' van.

Back at home, Charles went inside first. He found Buddy, took him upstairs to his room, and gave him a chew toy. "We have some new visitors," he told Buddy, giving him a special scratch between the ears. "Once they're settled in, you can come down and meet them, okay?"

Then he ran back downstairs in time to watch as Dad and Lizzie lowered the big box onto its side on the living room floor and opened the flaps. Maggie and Max were free to explore. The puppy came out first, carefully placing one big paw and then another onto the rug. She looked up at Charles, gave herself a shake, and plopped down on her pudgy backside. Then she opened her mouth in a big, drooly doggy smile and let out a deep "woof!"

Nice place! I like it here. Got any food for me and my little friend?

Maggie was mostly white, with big brown and black splotches, floppy brown ears, and a long, fluffy white tail. "Look!" said Lizzie. "Her paws are twice as big as Buddy's, even though she's way younger than he is!"

Charles and Lizzie and the Bean watched as Maggie got up again and started padding around, sniffing the couch, the Christmas tree, the coffee table, and the bookshelf. She was very curious and so, so cute.

But by the time the puppy had worked her way over to the fireplace, Max the kitten had crept partway out of the box. He began to yowl at his friend.

Too far! Too far! Don't leeeave meee!

Right away, Maggie galumphed back to the box and gave Max a big lick.

"Aww," sighed Mom. "She's such a good care-taker."

"Uh-oh," said the Bean. He was pointing toward the Christmas tree.

"Oh, no!" Charles saw that the kitten had gotten over being scared. As soon as Maggie had licked him, Max had started to charge around the living room, exploring at top speed. Now Charles watched as the kitten climbed up, up, up into the tree's branches, swatting at any ornaments that blocked his path. In a twinkling, Max was all the way up near the star. He paused and looked down when he heard Charles's voice, and his eyes grew big with fright.

CHAPTER THREE

Ohh, noo! How did I get all the way up heeeere? *Save meee, save meee!*

Max started mewing his heart out. Before any of the people in the room could move, Maggie jumped up, ran over to the tree, and put her paws on the bottom branches. The tree swayed this way and that, but it did not topple over. Maggie barked encouragingly as Max slowly clambered down.

That's it, that's it, little pal! Just one more branch and you're safe! Here, I'll make you a good target. Aim for that black spot on my back!

Finally, the kitten jumped off a lower branch, right onto his friend's broad back.

"Awesome!" Lizzie cried. She clapped her hands. "Did you guys know that Saint Bernard dogs are legendary rescuers? That's what they were trained to do, back in the mountains in Switzerland. When people got lost in a blizzard, Saint Bernards were sent out to find them."

Lizzie knew *everything* about dogs.

"Well, Maggie sure is living up to her heritage," Dad said.

Maggie and Max paraded proudly around the room several times before Max jumped off Maggie's back and began to scamper around on his own again. He dashed under the couch, then popped out and circled the Christmas tree three times. Then he flipped onto his back and started to swat at a low-hanging Christmas ornament.

Everybody laughed. Max certainly was a funny little guy.

Maggie watched calmly, woofing while the others laughed.

"He sure seems comfortable now!" said Dad, running over to rescue the glass ball.

"What a darling." Mom's voice was dreamy.

Charles and Lizzie looked at each other and rolled their eyes. Mom sure was in love with that kitten!

Over the next few days, *everyone* fell in love. Max was a little shy around Buddy at first, but soon both puppies and the kitten learned to play together. Charles loved to watch them tumble and chase. If only the Petersons could keep Max and Maggie forever! But Charles knew that was not going to happen. The Petersons were just a foster family for these two. They couldn't keep every animal that they took care of! The kitten and the puppy needed good homes, and Charles's job was to help find them.

There was only one problem. Ms. Dobbins had

been right: Maggie and Max did not like to be separated. If they were even in different rooms, Max would mew and mew, and Maggie would get very worried until she found him. "They're just a little frightened," Mom said. "I'm sure that if we give them enough love and attention, they will do fine on their own in their new homes." Like everybody else in the family, she knew it was not very likely that anybody would be willing to adopt a kitten *and* a puppy at the same time. Maggie and Max were going to have to learn to live without each other.

Charles couldn't wait to show off his new foster friends. He boasted about them at school. He invited Sammy over to meet them. And he told his Grandbuddy, Mrs. Peabody, all about Maggie and Max. Mrs. Peabody loved hearing about them, because she had once had a Saint Bernard of her own.

Charles wished his Scout friends could meet Maggie and Max, but there would be no den meetings for the next few weeks. Instead, the Scouts would be helping out at the Nest.

Mr. Baker came by the Petersons' house on Tuesday after supper to make sure that everything was set for the Scouts' visit to the Nest the next night. Charles was happy to introduce Maggie and Max.

"My, my!" Mr. Baker's eyes lit up when he saw the big puppy and her tiny playmate. "Aren't they something!" He sat right down on the floor and scooped Maggie into his arms. Right away, Maggie licked his face.

You're a very, very nice man. Want to be my friend?

Max used his sharp little claws to climb up Mr. Baker's knee and demand some attention, too.

Meee! Meee! Play with meee!

Mr. Baker laughed his deep, loud laugh. "What a pair!"

"They're available!" Lizzie said.

"Wouldn't you like to adopt them?" Charles asked. He thought Mr. Baker would make a fine pet owner. He obviously loved cats and dogs.

"I sure would," said Mr. Baker. "I miss having a cat. We had one who lived at the shelter, a big orange one with the greenest eyes you ever saw. Esmerelda. But one of our families fell in love with her, and I let them take her when they left to move into their new home."

"So?" Charles said. "That means you need a cat!"

"Maybe." Max was pushing his little head up against Mr. Baker's chin, which made him laugh again. "But a cat is one thing. A pesky kitten *plus* a gigantic puppy is another thing altogether. I'm very busy at the shelter, and I just don't have enough time to take responsibility for two animals." He thought for a moment. "Know what, though?"

Charles came over to pet Maggie. "What?"

"Maybe they could visit when you come to help out tomorrow night. We have a recreation room at the Nest where all the kids hang out. They run down there as soon as they're excused from dinner, while their parents are still eating. We don't have a TV — can't afford one, don't want one, anyway — and sometimes the kids get bored with doing puzzles and playing checkers."

"They wouldn't be bored with Maggie and Max around!" said Charles. "That's for sure."

"Well," Mom said, "that sounds wonderful. But we'll all be busy serving dinner in the dining room, won't we? Who would watch the pets?"

"No problem, Mom!" Lizzie spoke up. "I'll come along and keep an eye on Maggie and Max." Lizzie would do anything to help the Petersons' foster animals.

"So it's settled!" Mr. Baker was beaming. "We'll see you all tomorrow."

CHAPTER FOUR

"'Twas the night before Christmas," Sammy began, "and all through the house —"

"Not a creature was stirring, not even a mouse!" Charles jumped right in with the next line. He knew *that* one for sure.

Charles had come up with the brilliant idea of memorizing "The Night Before Christmas" to perform at the Nest on Christmas Eve. It was a classic poem — everybody had heard it a million times. Memorizing it would be a breeze! Especially if he and Sammy did it together, taking turns on each line. That way, Charles would only have to memorize *half* the poem! Even better, he'd really only have to *perform* half of it.

And instead of being alone onstage, he'd be with his best friend. The whole ordeal would be over in five minutes.

They were practicing in the Petersons' van, on the way over to the Nest. It was Wednesday, time for the Scouts' first visit to help out with dinner. Charles was a little nervous about meeting a whole bunch of new people. At least he wouldn't have to recite any poems *tonight*.

Dad was driving the van. Following them in the Petersons' red pickup truck were Mom, Lizzie, Maggie, and Max. The Bean was home with Steffi, his favorite babysitter, who always brought him "dog biscuits" (really bone-shaped oatmeal cookies) for a treat.

Charles knew that the kids at the Nest were going to love meeting the cuddly puppy and the funny little kitten. He was almost a little bit jealous, thinking about other kids getting to play with his foster pets. But he and Mom had talked about it a lot: how happy it would make the kids at the shelter, how Maggie and Max would enjoy meeting some new people, how it was good for the animals to get used to new places. Charles knew that was all true. Still, in a way, he was glad that he would be busy serving and cleaning up dinner so that he wouldn't have to *watch* Maggie lick some other kid's cheek, or see Max climb up onto someone else's shoulders.

Charles felt something jab into his ribs. It was Sammy's elbow. "Come on, Charles!" Sammy said. "Do your line!" He repeated his own. "The stockings were hung by the chimney with care. . . ."

"Hoping that Santa would come —" Charles had totally forgotten how it went. "Through the air?" he asked, scratching his head.

Sammy shook his head with disgust. "With hopes that Saint Nicholas soon would be there!" he proclaimed.

"Oh. Right." Charles was beginning to realize that he actually did not like this poem so much.

Who went around calling Santa Claus "Saint Nicholas," for one thing? Dumb. "Well, we're here!" he said, changing the subject. Dad had just pulled up in front of a big yellow house — big enough to fit *two* of the Petersons' houses inside. A wooden sign near the front door said: WELCOME TO THE NEST. The porch was decorated with Christmas lights and a big wreath.

Before Charles could even knock on the door, it opened wide. There was Mr. Baker, smiling down at the Scouts and laughing his big laugh as he bellowed, "Welcome, welcome!" and waved them all inside. Charles couldn't help noticing that Mr. Baker's big tummy kind of jiggled when he laughed. "Like a bowl full of jelly," Charles observed, remembering a scrap of the poem he was trying to learn. *That's* who Mr. Baker reminded him of: Santa Claus! Of course!

"You're just in time!" Mr. Baker said as the scouts came in. "The meatballs are simmering, the spaghetti is nearly done, and my homemade garlic bread is in the oven."

Charles took a big sniff. Sure enough, his mouth started to water. The smell of tomato sauce always made him hungry.

"Ah! And here are our furry friends." Mr. Baker smiled and waved at Mom and Lizzie, who were coming up the walk. Mom was carrying Max, all wrapped up in her favorite red wool scarf, and Maggie padded along next to Lizzie, showing off how well she walked on a leash. Mr. Baker laughed some more and clapped his hands. "Wonderful!" he crowed. "These two are going to be a huge hit." Mr. Baker turned to a gray-haired woman who was sitting at the reception desk just inside. "Miranda, will you show Lizzie and her animal friends to the rec room?"

"Gladly!" said Miranda. "Aren't they adorable? I just love cats, but unfortunately I can't live with one because I'm allergic."

Charles wanted to give Maggie and Max one

last pat, but before he knew it, Miranda had swept Lizzie, Max, and Maggie down the hall, talking all the time.

Mr. Baker gave the Scouts a quick tour of the Nest. "These are our offices, and here's the homework room, and here's the storage area where we keep extra clothing and blankets and other things that some families need when they come to stay with us." He pointed down a long hallway. "And down that way are the rooms where the families sleep and live, and down here," he said, leading the way down another hall, "is where we all have dinner!" He threw open two big doors and Charles saw a big dining room, more like a restaurant than a cafeteria. The tomato sauce smell was stronger than ever. People were already sitting at the tables: moms and dads and kids of all ages. Mr. Baker waved to the families as he led the Scouts back into the kitchen. "Come meet the guy in charge of all this," he said. He approached a man stirring a huge pot of sauce.

"Here are your helpers for tonight!" he announced. "Scouts, meet Danny. Danny, meet the Scouts."

"Excellent! I can always use some good help." Danny gave the Scouts a big smile. "Welcome aboard."

Charles liked Danny right away. He looked like a basketball player, tall and skinny and strong.

Danny tossed each Cub Scout a white paper chef's hat like his own. "All right, gentlemen," he said. "It's time to man your stations!"

Charles thought it would be cool to be on the other side of the cafeteria line. At school he slid his tray along and the lunch helpers served him. Now *he* was going to be the server. Each Scout would be dishing out a different part of the meal. Charles was excited when Danny assigned him and Sammy to the best spot of all: the meatball station! "I'm glad it's not the green beans," Sammy whispered. "I *hate* green beans."

Charles liked green beans okay, but he definitely

liked meatballs better. He was realizing that he should have eaten dinner before he came. The delicious smells were making him so hungry he could hardly stand it.

But he forgot all about being hungry once he started serving. "Two meatballs to a customer for starters," Danny had directed. "We might have enough for seconds, but we won't know until everyone's been served."

It felt good to be serving people food. Charles noticed that everybody smiled when they saw the meatballs. When he or Sammy carefully balanced two of them on top of the mound of spaghetti and sauce that the Scouts before them had served, people said "thank you" like they really *meant* it. Only one person didn't want any meatballs. "I'm a vegetarian," said a girl about Charles's age. "I don't eat any meat. But thanks, anyway." Charles split her meatballs between the girl's mom and her little brother.

Finally, everybody had been served. The dining

room was full of the sound of clinking forks and happy conversation. Charles noticed that several children had finished quickly, asked to be excused, and left the room. He could guess where *they* were headed.

"Bet those animals are getting lots of attention and love already!" Danny appeared behind Charles with another pan of meatballs. It was as if he was reading Charles's mind. "I heard about the kitten and puppy you brought to visit. Can't wait to meet them myself! Sure wish *I* could adopt a dog, but they don't allow pets where I live."

Fifteen minutes later, after Charles and Sammy had served a few latecomers, Danny came over again. "Good job, guys!" he said. "I bet you're ready for some dinner yourselves. Go ahead and grab some chow. I'll join you in the dining room in a minute."

Charles had just dug his fork into the biggest, juiciest, yummiest-looking meatball he'd ever seen, when Lizzie appeared at the door of the dining room. Charles saw that Maggie was with her, but where was Max? A little boy, the brother of that vegetarian girl, was helping to hold Maggie's leash. Maggie was whining and Charles thought she looked — well, *worried* was the only word for it.

"Mom! Dad!" Lizzie called. "Max is missing!"

CHAPTER FIVE

"Missing?" When Mom jumped up, her chair screeched back from the table. The whole dining room went quiet. Everybody was staring at the door, toward Lizzie and Maggie and the little boy.

"It's okay!" Dad jumped up, too. "Don't worry. Maggie will find him!"

Charles wasn't sure who Dad was talking to: Lizzie, or the rest of the people in the dining room. But it seemed to help. Lizzie nodded and tried to smile, and the diners went back to their spaghetti and conversation.

All but Charles and Sammy. After one wistful look at his meatballs, Charles got up and headed for the door, with his best friend right behind him. If Max was lost, they had to help find him, no

36

matter *how* hungry they might be. After all, he was only a little tiny kitten.

"Where did you see him last?" Mom was asking Lizzie questions as the search party — Mom, Dad, Charles, Sammy, the little boy, and, of course Maggie — hurried down the hall, back toward the recreation room. "Which way do you think he went? Have you tried letting Maggie search for him?"

"Actually," the little boy said, in a very serious voice, "we weren't paying much attention to him for a few minutes. Lizzie was demonstrating how to teach Maggie to shake hands."

Mom smiled at the boy. "What's your name?" she asked.

"Actually, it's Evan."

Evan was very young — maybe five years old. But when he talked he seemed older. Charles thought he had a pretty good vocabulary for a kindergartner. He smiled at Evan, but Evan didn't smile back. Instead, he bit his lip as if he was about to cry. "Don't worry," Charles told Evan. "We'll find Max."

Just then, Mr. Baker bustled up. "I hear one of our guests has gone missing." He wasn't laughing, for a change.

Evan nodded. "Max ran away! We have to find him. He's the best kitten ever. Actually, I *love* Max! He's so entertaining!"

"Well, now." Mr. Baker knelt down to look into Evan's eyes. "I doubt anybody let him outside, and the Nest isn't *that* big. Don't worry, Evan. I'm sure we can find him." He stood up and shook his head. "Poor little guy. Hope he's not scared. Funny — I was just thinking that perhaps we could adopt him here, after all. If he can be separated from his partner, that is!" He reached down and patted Maggie.

Evan's face lit up when he heard that, and Lizzie and Charles grinned at each other. Excellent. Maybe they'd already found a home for one of their foster pets. Then they both lost their smiles. Before they could think about finding Max a home, they had to *find* Max.

At that moment, Maggie stopped in her tracks. Her ears went up and her tail stuck straight out. She sniffed the air and cocked her head as if she were listening hard. Then she sniffed again. And she began to whine.

My friend! He's nearby! I know that smell. I know that sound. Follow me! We have to find that little guy, right now!

Maggie pulled on her leash, dragging Lizzie along as she dashed down the hall, turned a corner, and galloped down another hall. She was barking and whining as she ran. Evan grabbed Charles's hand and pulled him along. Everybody ran after Maggie. Then the big puppy skidded to a stop in front of a closed door, and everybody gathered around her.

"That's my family's room!" Evan told Charles.

"Where my mom and dad and my sisters and me sleep!"

Mr. Baker knocked on the door. Nobody answered. Maggie barked and whined some more.

He's in there! My little friend is in there! Let us in! Let us in!

Mr. Baker knocked again. No answer. Everybody groaned.

"What's going on?" asked a woman who had just come up behind Charles.

"Mom!" Evan said. "I think Max is in our room!"

Evan's mom raised an eyebrow. But she didn't ask any questions. She just stepped forward and unlocked the door. "I was just here, to get a sweater," she was saying. "If there was a kitten in the room, wouldn't I have seen him?"

Maggie pushed past her. The pup ran straight

over to a tall dresser against one wall. She jumped up, put both paws on the top drawer, and barked.

In here! In here! My friend is stuck inside! Somebody help!

Evan's mom was staring at Maggie. "My goodness!" she said. "That's the drawer I took my sweater out of. What's going on here?" She pulled the drawer open — and Max leaped out! The tiny black kitten was meowing at the top of his little lungs.

It's about tiiiime! It was dark in there! I was scaaaared!

"Max! Max!" Evan yelled. Maggie was already licking her little friend. Evan got down on the floor and hugged both animals at the same time.

Evan's mom shook her head. "The kitten must have jumped in there when my back was turned."

"Fortunately, Maggie knew just exactly where to find him," Evan said. "Actually, she's a hero." Now Maggie was licking *his* face. Evan looked so happy, snuggling with the kitten and the puppy.

"She sure is," Charles agreed. "That makes *two* rescues for Maggie." He told Evan and his mom about how Maggie had helped Max get down from the Christmas tree.

While Evan patted Maggie some more, Charles looked around the room. There was a set of bunk beds along one wall, and a big bed, for Evan's parents, against another. Two dressers, one comfy chair, and a small table filled the rest of the space.

Charles tried to imagine how it would feel to have lost his own house, and to have to live in one small room with his family. It would not be easy. But having a friendly animal to cuddle sure would make it feel more like home.

CHAPTER SIX

"All the kids *loved* Max and Maggie." That night at home, Lizzie was telling Charles about her time in the recreation room at the Nest. "They loved that Maggie was so big and friendly and soft and warm. They all wanted to hug and kiss and cuddle with her, and she let them. She is so patient and sweet." Lizzie scratched Maggie's ears and gave her a hug. "Aren't you, Maggie?"

Mmmm, I just love kissing and cuddling! The more the better! And I LOVE having my ears scratched!

Then Lizzie looked at Max, who was pretending that a dust ball under the kitchen table was a mouse.

He stalked it with a twitching tail, then pounced. The dust ball was history. Max meowed with pride.

I'm a mighty hunter! Watch out for meee!

"And they loved that Max is so funny and playful. He kept all the kids laughing — until he disappeared on us, that is!"

Max finished teaching the dust ball a lesson and began to stalk the red Christmas ribbon that Charles was dangling in front of him.

"I wish they could both go live at the Nest, but Mr. Baker said 'no way,'" Charles told his sister. He pulled the ribbon along the floor, and Max dashed after it, batting at the curly ends with his paws. "He said maybe the Nest could adopt Max, but only if we can make sure that he can get along without Maggie."

"That's the hard part," Lizzie said. "They're such good friends. They hate to be separated."

By then, Max had gotten bored with the ribbon.

He ambled over to Maggie, curled up against the curve of her belly, and closed his eyes for a nap.

Charles remembered something Mom had said when Max and Maggie first arrived, about the kitten and puppy being a little frightened and needing lots of love and attention. "Maybe we just have to show them that they can each be safe and happy on their own," he said. "They're so used to being together that they don't know any other way. But we can teach them."

"Good idea." Lizzie almost looked surprised, like nobody but her ever had good ideas. "But how?"

Charles glanced at Maggie and Max, all curled up together. They looked so cozy. "What if I take Maggie into my room to sleep tonight, and you take Max into yours? They'll be right next door to each other, and each of them will be with a person who is giving them lots of attention. It will be a start, anyway."

Lizzie nodded. "Okay, but why do you get to choose who goes where? What if I want Maggie?"

"It was my idea!" Charles could tell Lizzie wished *she'd* thought of it. He didn't really care whether he had Maggie or Max, but now he was going to stick with what he'd said.

"What about Buddy?" Lizzie asked.

"He's already fast asleep in the Bean's room," Charles told her. "He's happy there." Usually Charles was jealous when Buddy slept in his little brother's room. But for tonight it was a good thing.

Charles scooped up a sleepy Maggie, and Lizzie picked up Max. They headed for the stairs. "Good night!" Charles called to his parents, who were reading in the living room by the fireplace.

"Good night?" Mom looked up from her book. "You mean, I don't have to nag you two about bedtime for once?" She waved Lizzie over so she could give Max a good-night pat and a kiss. She sure did love that kitten.

"We're being extra good so Santa will bring us lots of loot," Lizzie said.

Dad just raised an eyebrow.

Upstairs, Lizzie paused near her door. She took Max's paw and made it wave. "Good night, Maggie!" she said in a meowy voice.

"Good night, Max," Charles said back, in a woofy voice. He made Maggie's paw wave back. "Sleep tight, little pal!"

Charles put on his pj's and climbed into bed. Maggie seemed perfectly content, curled up near Charles's feet. But just as Charles was beginning to drift off to sleep, Maggie jumped up and let out a soft "woof!"

"What?" Charles asked sleepily. He reached out to pat Maggie. "It's okay," he told her. "Go back to sleep."

But Maggie did not go back to sleep. Maggie barked again.

How can I sleep? My little friend needs me! I can hear him crying!

Charles sat up and listened. Now he could hear a faint meowing coming from Lizzie's room. It almost sounded as if Max was calling Maggie's name.

Maggieeee! Maggieeee!

So that was it! Max was calling for his friend. But Charles knew that Max was really safe and sound with Lizzie.

"It's okay," he said again. He gathered Maggie into his arms. "Time to sleep. Your friend is fine." He used the soothing voice that Dad always used when Charles woke up scared after a bad dream. Charles knew that Lizzie was probably doing the same thing in *her* room, with Max.

It was a long, restless night. Maggie kept jumping up, but every time Charles just patted her and hugged her and told her everything was fine. When his Snoopy alarm went off in the morning, Charles stretched and yawned. Then he looked down at the end of his bed and saw Maggie, curled up in a ball and sleeping soundly. Finally!

That was the first night. It took two more nights, and lots of practice during the day, for Max and Maggie to get used to being apart. But finally, all the Petersons agreed that Max was ready to be on his own. By Saturday morning, the little kitten could play and sleep and eat even if Maggie was nowhere in sight — and Maggie didn't seem quite as worried about her friend. Max and Maggie had learned that it was okay to be apart, and that meant that Max was ready to go to his new home at the Nest.

On Saturday, Mom drove Charles and Max to the Nest. "Here he is!" Charles handed the cat carrier over to Mr. Baker. "Take good care of him!"

"I promise," said Mr. Baker. "This is wonderful. The kids are going to be so happy to have a kitten!"

Mom looked a little sad on the way home. "It

sure was nice having a cat around," she said. "I'll miss that little guy."

Maggie must have felt the same way. First she padded all through every room in the house, looking for Max. Then, finally, she seemed to understand that Max wasn't just in the next room this time. This time, he was really gone. Maggie spent the rest of the day lying under the Christmas tree with her head resting on her paws, heaving long sighs and watching the Petersons with her sad brown eyes. Maggie's big heart was obviously broken.

CHAPTER SEVEN

"When what to my wondering eyes should appear, but a miniature sleigh and eight tiny reindeer!" Sammy said his line and waited for Charles to say the next one.

And waited.

Charles was thinking. "Why do they say eight *tiny* reindeer?" he asked. "If they're so tiny, how can they pull Santa's sled? Maybe it's because his *sleigh* is miniature — that means little, right? But how little can it be? It's loaded with presents for every kid in the world!"

"Charles," Sammy said. "It's just a poem." He gave Maggie a hug. "Tell him to just say his line, Maggie." The boys were at Charles's house, practicing their poem. Maggie was still moping, and Buddy was trying to cheer her up by rolling onto his back and batting at her chin with his paws, the way Max always did. But Buddy was not Max, and Maggie knew it. Max was gone, and nobody could take his place. Maggie let out one of her big sighs and plodded over to lie down by the Christmas tree.

Charles *couldn't* say his line, because he couldn't quite remember it. And, even worse, he knew the hardest lines of all were still coming up, the ones where Santa calls to his reindeer by name. No matter how hard he tried, Charles could not get those reindeer names straight. Dasher and Dancer, he could remember. But after that he got all mixed up. Comet? Cupid? What kind of names were those for reindeer?

"You know what, Sammy?"

"What?"

"I really do not like this poem." Charles buried his face in the soft fur of Buddy's neck. "Maybe we have to come up with another idea for the Nest's Christmas show. This isn't working out."

Sammy shrugged. "It's okay with me if we do something else," he said. "But it's up to you to think of it."

"Maybe we could just sing 'Jingle Bells' or something," Charles suggested. He knew it was a dumb idea, but at the moment it was the only one he could think of.

Sammy rolled his eyes. "You can do better than *that*." He went over to give Maggie a hug. But the big puppy struggled out of his arms and galloped toward the front door, woofing her big loud woof and waving her big feathery tail.

You're back! You're back! Oh, my dear little friend. I'm so glad you came back! I missed you so much!

Sammy looked at Charles. Charles looked at Sammy. What was going on?

Then the doorbell rang.

"Can you get that, Charles?" Mom called from the kitchen.

Charles was already on his way, with Buddy trotting beside him. Sammy grabbed onto Maggie's collar to keep her inside while Charles pulled the door open. There, on the porch, was Mr. Baker, holding a cat carrier. He did not look very jolly.

"Mr. Baker!" Charles said.

"Hello, Charles," replied Mr. Baker. "Can you guess why I'm here?"

By then, Maggie had struggled out of Sammy's grasp. She had both big paws up on the cat carrier. Her tail was wagging and she was woofing softly. Charles could hear happy meows coming from inside the carrier. He recognized that voice. It was Max.

Hooraaaay, hooraaaay! I'm back to staaaay!

"What happened?" Charles asked.

"Let's just say it didn't work out," said Mr. Baker.

Mom came into the hall, wiping her hands on a kitchen towel. "Oh, dear," she said. She took the cat carrier from Mr. Baker and knelt down to open it up. "Hello, cutie-pie!" She reached inside for the kitten. But Max dashed straight past her toward Maggie. His purr rumbled loudly enough for everyone to hear as he twined himself around Maggie's legs, pushing the top of his head up against her chin. Maggie wagged her tail and made soft whuffing noises as she gave Max a few huge, happy licks.

"That's the first time he stopped meowing since you dropped him off with me on Saturday," said Mr. Baker. "He never stopped crying for his friend. Evan and the other kids tried everything to distract him, but nothing worked. He didn't want to play with string, or chase toy mice, or eat kitty treats, or anything. He just ignored the kids and paced up and down, crying and crying. I guess he just missed Maggie too much." He shook his head. "It's a pity. The kids are heartbroken. They've really fallen in love with this kitten."

"I can understand that," Mom said.

"Maybe you just have to adopt Maggie at the Nest, too!" Charles was still hoping that Mr. Baker would change his mind about that.

But Mr. Baker shook his head. "I just can't see how I can handle a puppy *and* a kitten. But I know everybody would be very, very happy if you brought them both to visit again this week."

"We'd be glad to," said Mom.

"And Charles, maybe you could spend your volunteer time in the recreation room instead of the dining room," Mr. Baker suggested. "You can help out Beverly, our rec room coordinator. She said Evan asked especially for you to be there. He said you are — uh, let's see — 'actually a really cool dude!'"

"Ha!" Sammy snorted.

Charles looked at his friend. "You're just

jealous," he said. "You're going to be ladling out meatballs again, and I get to hang out with Maggie and Max and the kids." Secretly, Charles felt flattered to know that Evan thought he was a really cool dude. But would he still think so if Charles couldn't remember his lines for the holiday show?

CHAPTER EIGHT

"Charles! Charles!" Evan started jumping up and down the minute Charles walked into the Nest's recreation room. "Guess what? I made a picture of Maggie and Max." Before Charles could even introduce himself to Beverly, Evan had grabbed his hand and pulled him over to a bulletin board. "See? There's Maggie. She's discovering Max in my mommy's sweater drawer."

Charles looked at the red-and-yellow scribbling, trying to make sense of it. "Oh, sure!" he said. "There's Maggie, right?"

Evan laughed. "No, silly! That's Mommy. Maggie's over there." He pointed to a green scribble.

Now Charles could see that the scribble looked sort of like it had a tail. "Great picture, Evan!"

"You must be Charles." Beverly came over to say hello. "I've heard a lot about you, and, of course I met your sister Lizzie last week. Welcome!"

Charles smiled at her, but Evan was tugging on his hand again.

"Where *is* Maggie?" Evan asked. "Where's Max? Aren't they coming? I thought they were coming tonight!"

"They're coming, they're coming." Charles had ridden over to the Nest with Dad and the Scouts. Mom drove behind them in the pickup with Maggie and Max. "In fact," Charles went on, "I think I hear them right now."

"Yay!" Evan shouted. He ran to the door.

"Evan, don't forget to use your indoor voice," called Beverly. "The animals will be scared if you yell." She turned to Charles. "He's so excited to see them that he ate dinner early so he could be here when they arrived. I'm excited, too! We haven't had so much fun in the rec room since the Easter Bunny came to visit. We just *love* Maggie and Max." She frowned. "It's just too bad it didn't work out to have Max here by himself. He sure did miss his pal!"

"I know," Charles said. "Maggie missed him, too. She was really sad without her friend. I guess we have to keep working on that separation thing."

Beverly made a *tsk-tsk* sound. "It's a shame they can't find a place together," she said. "I'd love to have them both here, but I have my hands full already watching all the kids. I can't take care of two animals, too."

"They're here!" Evan shouted.

Maggie galloped into the room, pulling Mom behind her. Mom was struggling to hold on to Maggie's leash, while Max climbed up her coat and perched on her shoulder.

"Close the door, Evan!" said Beverly. "Let's keep these two critters safe."

Evan slammed the door shut and ran over to throw his arms around Maggie.

"Hello, Beverly!" Mom unstuck Max's claws from her collar and handed the kitten to Charles. "Keep an eye on this one," she told him. "I'm going to help serve dinner. I'll be back soon."

As soon as Charles put Max down, he scampered over to join Evan and Maggie.

"Look at Evan," Beverly whispered to Charles. "He's so happy!"

It was true. Charles saw Evan's smile grow huge as he patted first Maggie and then Max. The puppy and the kitten looked happy, too. They were together, and they were getting plenty of pats. Maggie's barks and Max's meows were like a sweet duet.

Maggie rolled over onto her back.

This is the life! Rub my tummy some more, would you? How about another kiss? And maybe you could scratch my ears? Don't forget to give my little friend some attention, too!

Max rolled over just like Maggie and batted his paws at Evan.

Wheee! Pat meee!

After a few minutes, more kids started to arrive. They all ran over to see the pets. "I want to walk Maggie!" said one girl. "I want to play with Max!" said another. Charles recognized Evan's sister from last week. Suddenly, Max and Maggie were surrounded by a circle of kids.

It was too much for the little kitten. Max dashed between a boy's legs and ran over to Charles. His eyes were wide with fear.

Eeeek! Save meeeee!

Charles scooped up the scared little kitten.

Then Maggie dashed over to be near her friend. She leaned her big body against Charles.

There are too many people in here! Somebody just stuck his finger in my ear! What if my little friend gets hurt?

Charles looked over at Beverly. "They love attention," he told her. "But maybe this is too *much* attention at once." He wondered if this was why Max had run away to hide in a drawer last week.

"Good point." Beverly nodded. "Okay, kids, we're going to give the animals some space. How about if we take turns petting and walking them? And while you're waiting your turn, you can draw pictures of our new friends."

Quickly, Beverly organized the kids into groups. When Mr. Baker stopped in a few minutes later, one pair of kids was taking Maggie on a walk down the hall while another pair was sitting on the couch with Max, playing "chase the shoelace" with the kitten. The rest of the kids were seated at a long table, drawing happily with markers and crayons.

"This is great," Charles heard Beverly tell Mr. Baker. "Walking the puppy helps teach the kids responsibility, even if they *are* only going as far as the dining room. And Max sure does make the kids laugh. He seems happy, as long as he knows Maggie is nearby."

After Mr. Baker left, Charles tried to keep an eye on both Max and Maggie and also pay attention to Evan, who was drawing a picture of Maggie helping Santa Claus deliver presents. "See?" Evan asked, pointing to a red blob. "That's Santa. He's standing on the roof at my house, looking down the chimney."

Charles was trying to figure out which scribble was the chimney, when, suddenly, Evan burst into tears. "I don't *have* a house anymore since the fire," he wailed, as if he'd just remembered. "How is Santa going to find me?"

Charles couldn't blame Evan for crying. He thought about the Petersons' Christmas tree at home, with all the familiar decorations, and the big red stockings that said CHARLES, LIZZIE, and BEAN, already hung by the fireplace, and the green vase full of holly that Mom always put on the table in the hall. Christmas just wouldn't be Christmas without those things.

Charles gave Evan a hug. "Santa will find you," he said. "I'm sure of it. He's a really smart guy, you know."

Evan's sobs had died down to sniffles when, suddenly, Charles heard somebody yell, "Hey! Where's that kitten?"

CHAPTER NINE

"You are really something else," Charles said as he gave Max a quick scratch under the chin. The kitten purred and pushed against Charles's hand.

It was the next afternoon, and Charles was sitting in the living room by the fireplace, helping Lizzie make paper chains for the tree. He wasn't sure why she thought it was important to make more paper chains, since there were already dozens of them on the tree.

"They're all old and faded," Lizzie had said. "We need new ones."

So, they were making paper chains. Charles was cutting out strips of green and red paper, and Lizzie was taping them into circle shapes, linking the circles together as she went. Dad had taken the Bean along while he did some Christmas shopping, and Buddy had jumped into Dad's red pickup with them. Charles had a feeling that Buddy needed a break from Max and Maggie, who had kind of taken over the whole house.

Mom was upstairs in her study, working on a newspaper story about a farmer who was giving away Christmas trees to anyone who needed one. "It's due at five o'clock," she had said. "And I'm only on paragraph one. Please keep an eye on Max and Maggie, and don't interrupt me unless our house is on fire!" She'd paused on her way up the stairs. "Actually, if the house is on fire, call nine-one-one first, so your dad and the other firefighters will come. Then come knock on my door."

"Gotcha," said Charles.

"Hey!" Lizzie pulled a strip of paper away from Max. "Cut that out, you pest!" But she was laughing.

Charles pulled Maggie onto his lap for a hug. He had never met such a huggable puppy. Maggie was almost like one of those gigantic, floppy stuffed dogs you could hug forever. She never struggled to get down, the way Buddy sometimes did. She just settled in, her big paws resting on either side of Charles's neck in a warm puppy hug. She was so heavy that sometimes Charles's legs fell asleep when she lay on his lap too long!

Ahh, very comfortable. I think I'll take a nap. Hey! What's going on?

Charles had to stretch out in order to grab another piece of green construction paper, which made Maggie slide off his lap.

Oh, well. Guess I might as well play a while, as long as I'm up. Where's my favorite pal?

Maggie yawned as she trotted over to Max and gave him a big, sloppy lick. She bowed down with her butt in the air and her paws stretched out in front. Then she turned and, looking over her shoulder, trotted off.

Try to catch me, my little friend!

Max rolled over and jumped up and ran after Maggie, all in one second. He was like a flash of black-and-white, streaking toward the stairs.

Wheee! Wait for meeee!

"Oh, no, the stair game." Lizzie rolled her eyes. Charles could tell that even Lizzie was beginning to feel a little overwhelmed by having two foster pets at once. The Petersons really had to do something about finding homes for Max and Maggie, together or separate. If they were still there by Christmas — which was only a week away! — Mom might insist that she had really had enough and that Max and Maggie would have to leave. *Then* where would they go?

Personally, Charles was enjoying having a puppy and kitten as visitors. They were so entertaining. Take the stair game. It was something Max and Maggie had invented all by themselves. Max would run up the stairs and meow at the top of his little lungs from the landing. From below, Maggie would bark in answer. Then Maggie would lumber up to the top of the stairs, and Max would scamper down. Maggie would bark, and Max would meow. Over and over and over. Charles wasn't sure exactly what the *point* of the game was, but it was obvious that the kitten and puppy were having a great time.

First Charles heard meowing. He couldn't see the landing from where he sat, but he could tell by the sound that Max was at the top of the stairs.

Hee-hee! Come and get meeee!

Then he heard barking.

You just wait, little friend! I'm coming after you!

Charles heard Maggie clamber up the stairs. *Thump, thump, thump.* But before she made it to the landing, Charles heard Max dash down. *Tooka-tooka-took.* His little paws moved twice as fast as the big puppy's.

Max meowed some more, from the bottom of the stairs.

Hee-hee-hee! Missed meeee! Come and get meeee!

From above, Maggie barked.

Think you're funny, do you, little friend? I'll get you next time! Hey! Wait a second! What's going on? Help! I'm stuck! I'm stuck! Do something! Help!

Charles shook his head as he cut a pile of green strips. That Maggie sure could bark a lot! Suddenly, Max raced into the room. He jumped onto Charles's lap and started meowing and kneading his sharp claws into Charles's leg.

Help! My friend needs help! Saaave her! Pleeease!

"Ouch!" said Charles. "What are you doing?"

Max jumped off Charles's lap and ran to the bottom of the stairs. Then he ran back toward Charles and Lizzie. Then he ran back to the stairs. Maggie was still barking.

Charles looked at Lizzie. "I think something's wrong."

They both jumped up, ran into the front hall, and stared up the stairs. "Oh, no!" groaned Charles.

There, on the landing, was Maggie. She stared down at them sadly and gave one last whiny bark.

Her head was caught between two railings. She was trying to back herself out, but Charles could see right away that she was stuck.

Just at that moment, Mom came out of her study. "What is going *on* out here?" she began. "I thought I asked you two —" Then she stopped. "Oh, no!"

It took all the Petersons (Dad came home the second Mom called him on his cell phone) plus one saw (borrowed from Sammy's dad next door) to get Maggie unstuck. Everybody agreed that Max was a hero, just like his puppy friend.

"Maggie is usually the one who saves Max!" Charles said. "But this time, Max saved Maggie by letting us know she was trapped. They really are best friends." He had Max on his lap, and Lizzie was comforting Maggie on hers.

"And they really do belong together," Dad said thoughtfully. "I call a Peterson powwow, right this minute. I think we should make a family decision that these two animals *have* to find a home together. We can't separate friends as good as these. Agreed?"

"Agreed!" everyone chorused.

"But where in the world will that home be?" asked Mom as she reached out to pet Max. "I can't imagine."

Charles could. In fact, he had a pretty good idea of the *perfect* home for Max and Maggie. But he first he had to convince somebody else that he was right.

CHAPTER TEN

"What are you so happy about?" Sammy asked Charles. "You keep smiling. C'mon. Tell me!"

Charles shook his head. "You'll find out."

"I better," said Sammy. "And you owe me a humongous favor for agreeing to recite 'The Night Before Christmas' all by myself."

It was Christmas Eve, and the boys were in the back of the van, on their way to the Nest along with the other Scouts. Charles *was* happy. He had been working hard all week, but it was worth it. He had solved two big problems. One: how to find a home for a puppy and a kitten that could not be separated; and two: how to find a poem he could memorize for tonight's showcase.

The second problem was the easiest. Charles had figured out that if he wrote his *own* poem, he wouldn't have such a hard time remembering it. He didn't even have to figure out the form for the poem. He just used "The Night Before Christmas" as a model but changed the words, the same way the Cub Scouts changed the words of familiar songs like "It's a Small World." Charles thought the poem had turned out pretty well. Maybe he would be a writer someday, like his mother.

He would have liked to teach the poem to Sammy, but he'd only finished it the night before. Anyway, that would ruin the surprise, which had to do with problem one. And Charles wanted *everyone* to be surprised, including his own family, the families at the Nest, and all the Scouts. Well, there was *one* person who was in on the surprise. But that person wasn't telling, either.

The Petersons' van pulled up at the Nest at the same time Lizzie, Mom, and the Bean arrived with Max and Maggie. The Scouts piled out of the van, excited to be at the Nest on Christmas Eve. Charles went over to help his mom and ended up carrying Max up the front walk while Lizzie walked Maggie. The door swung open before Dad could even ring the bell.

"They're here!" shouted Evan. "Merry Christmas, Max! Merry Christmas, Maggie! Merry Christmas, Charles! Merry Christmas, Charles's family!"

Behind him, Mr. Baker laughed. "And Merry Christmas to all our Scout friends, too," he said. "We have really enjoyed having you boys here every week. Come in, come in!"

The Nest was warm and bright with Christmas lights that draped all around the front desk and led down the hall. It smelled good, too. Like turkey and stuffing and — Charles took a big sniff. "Apple pie?" he asked Mr. Baker.

"You bet! Made it myself." Mr. Baker patted Charles on the shoulder. "How about if you and I get Max and Maggie settled in the rec room?

Lizzie, we could use your help in the dining room tonight, okay?"

Lizzie shrugged. "Sure!" She handed Maggie's leash to Mr. Baker and followed Mom and Dad and the Scouts down the hall.

"So, is everything all set?" Mr. Baker asked Charles in a low voice as they walked with the animals toward the rec room.

Charles nodded. "All set!"

"Excellent." Mr. Baker pushed open the door to the rec room, and Beverly came over to welcome the animals. "You won't have many visitors tonight, Bev," Mr. Baker said. "At least not once the showcase gets going."

"Fine with me," Beverly answered. "Maggie and Max and I have some catching up to do, anyway."

Charles gave the puppy and kitten each a quick pat, then followed Mr. Baker to the dining room. Sammy was waiting for him by the mashed-potatoes station. "Ready to tell yet?" he asked as Charles took his place.

Charles just shook his head and pretended to zip his lips.

Dinner went by in a blur, and before he knew it, Charles was helping to move tables aside and set up chairs. In a few minutes, the dining room had been converted into a theater, with rows of chairs facing a platform where the performers would appear.

Charles felt his hands getting sweaty. He gulped. All too soon, he would be up there on that platform, performing in front of a whole bunch of people! He took a deep breath and tried to relax. After all, these people weren't strangers anymore. He'd been serving them food for weeks now, and he'd gotten to know most of the Nest's residents pretty well — especially the kids, of course.

Before they let the audience in, Mr. Baker stood up in front of all the volunteers and explained how the showcase would work. The performers would sit in the back row. He would introduce each one in turn, and they would come up onstage and do their thing, then go back and sit down. At the end of the evening, everybody would come up onstage together for one last bow. "Are we ready?" Mr. Baker asked. He went and opened the doors, the audience flooded in and found their seats, and the showcase began.

Sammy was third, after a Scout who sang "Silent Night" and a funny skit by Charles's mom and dad. Charles was impressed by how well his friend recited "The Night Before Christmas." Sammy didn't make one mistake! Charles gave him a high five when he got back to his seat. Then they sat together and watched all the other volunteers perform. The audience loved everything!

Then Charles saw Mr. Baker look at him and give a secret wink. As Charles made his way to the front of the room, Mr. Baker disappeared, slipping out through a side door.

For a second, standing up there in front of everyone, Charles felt his hands go all sweaty. His knees felt like Jell-O. But then he looked out at the audience and spotted Evan, who smiled and waved. Charles took a deep breath. "Hi, everybody! Merry Christmas! I wrote a special poem, just for tonight." His voice was a little squeaky, so he cleared his throat. "Um, so here it is." Then he began.

> "'Twas the night before Christmas,
> A time to be glad,
> But inside the Nest
> Lots of people were sad.
>
> They lay awake wishing
> That Santa would say,
> 'Merry Christmas to all!
> Max and Maggie can stay!'

But that wouldn't happen,
As everyone knew.
If one pet was a handful,
How could they keep two?

Mr. Baker's so busy,
With the Nest in his care,
He can't handle one pet,
Much less have a pair.

Danny loves dogs
But he doesn't have space
And he isn't allowed
To keep pets in his place.

Miranda loves cats
But their fur brings on sneezing —
And how could she answer
The phone if she's wheezing?

Beverly's got
All the kids in her care —
Just think of the noise
With two animals there!

But wait! Look outside —
Can you hear Santa's call?
He's bringing the Nest
the best present of all . . ."

Just then Mr. Baker reappeared in the door-
way — but now he was dressed up like Santa, in
a red suit and a very obvious fake white beard!
He walked down the aisle, leading Maggie on her
bright red Christmas leash. Maggie carried a big
red-and-white-striped knitted stocking in her
mouth — and in the stocking was Max, his bright
eyes looking all around.

The audience broke into excited whispers
and giggles. From the stage, Charles saw Evan's

face light up when he saw his favorite animal friends.

Soon Mr. Baker was standing next to Charles. They smiled at each other. Now it was Mr. Baker's turn to finish the poem. He faced the audience and began.

"I thought and I thought
To come up with a way
For our dear Max and Maggie
To come here to stay.

Two pets are a handful
For one person, it's true.
But with everyone's help,
Look at all we can do!

Beverly, Danny,
Miranda, and me,
We'll pitch in together
To make it easy, you see.

The kids can help, too,
Each night and each day —
So, Merry Christmas to all!
Max and Maggie can stay!"

For a second, the whole room was quiet. Then the audience burst into cheers and applause. Suddenly, Charles felt almost as if he might start crying, so he quickly knelt down and threw his arms around Maggie's big, furry neck. Charles could hardly believe he had finally gotten Mr. Baker to change his mind. It had taken a lot of work to convince him, but Mr. Baker had finally understood that if everyone at the Nest pitched in, they could take care of both a puppy and a kitten.

"I think you've both found a wonderful home," Charles whispered to Maggie and Max. "Merry Christmas."

Puppy Tips

Holidays are so much fun — but they can be dangerous for pets! With all the excitement going on, it's especially important to take good care of your dog.

There are lots of unfamiliar things to play with and eat at holiday times. Your pet can get an upset stomach if she eats holiday table scraps that are too rich. Some holiday plants, like poinsettias and holly, can make dogs very sick if they eat a leaf or a berry. You might think chocolate would make a nice special treat, but it is poisonous for dogs, too. Tinsel, wrapping paper, ribbons: none of these make healthy treats for a curious pup, so keep them tidied away when your dog is on the loose.

Dogs aren't happy when their routines change, so try to walk and feed your pet at the same time each day. And don't forget to hug your dog and give her lots of attention, even when you're busy!

Dear Reader,

In my family, the pets always get Christmas gifts along with the people. I usually give my brother's cats a fun new toy, and my brother and his family give my dog some yummy treats.

It's fun to pick out a present for your pet — but don't leave it under the tree, or your pet might open it before he's supposed to!

Happy Holidays to all my animal friends!

Yours from the Puppy Place,
Ellen Miles

THE SECRETS OF DROON

By Tony Abbott

Read them all!

Under the stairs, a magical world awaits you!

Available wherever books are sold.

■ SCHOLASTIC

A Little Sister Can Be A Big Pain– Especially If She Has Magical Powers!

Can it be true? Adorable, annoying five-year-old Violet actually has magical powers? For eight-year-old Mabel, being a big sister will never be the same.

Mabel knows being a big sister has a power all its own. But when Violet conjures up a pool, Mabel doesn't know how she will explain it to the neighbors—or her parents!

SCHOLASTIC
www.scholastic.com

SISMAG18